American edition published in 1999 by Carolrhoda Books, Inc.,
by arrangement with Bloomsbury Publishing, Plc., London, England.

Text copyright © 1999 by Adrienne Geoghegan
Illustrations copyright © 1999 Adrian Johnson

Carolrhoda Books, Inc., a division of The Lerner Publishing Group
241 First Avenue North, Minneapolis, MN 55401 U.S.A.

Website address: www.lernerbooks.com

Library of Congress Cataloging-in-Publication Data

Geoghegan, Adrienne.
There's a Wardrobe in My Monster! / by Adrienne Geoghegan :
illustrated by Adrian Johnson.
p.   cm.
Summary: Bored with her ordinary pets, a young girl chooses a monster from
the pet store, but soon finds that it is more trouble than she expected.
ISBN 1-57505-414-0 (alk. paper)
[1. Monsters—Fiction. 2. Pets—Fiction.] I. Johnson, Adrian, ill. II. Title.
PZ7.G2927Th 1999 [E]—dc21
99-19086

Printed and Bound in Belgium
1 2 3 4 5 6 04 03 02 01 00 99

THERE'S A WARDROBE IN MY MONSTER!

Adrienne Geoghegan and Adrian Johnson

Carolrhoda Books, Inc., Minneapolis

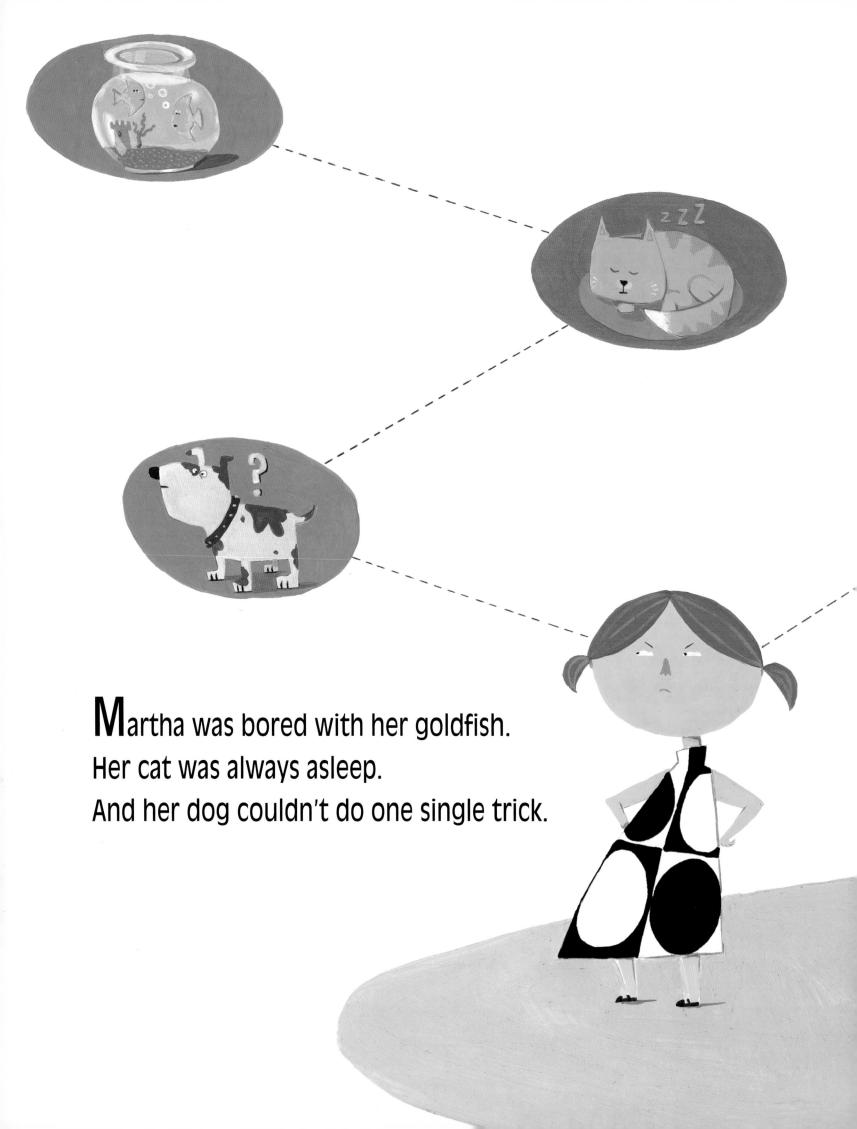

Martha was bored with her goldfish.
Her cat was always asleep.
And her dog couldn't do one single trick.

"What I want is a monster," she said. "A naughty, wicked, great big ugly monster." So she marched into the nearest pet shop in town with all her piggy-bank savings.

"One large monster, please," she said quite boldly.

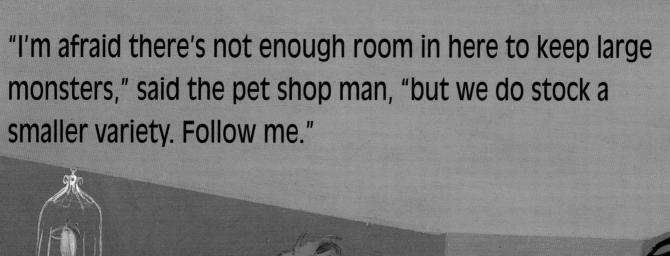

"I'm afraid there's not enough room in here to keep large monsters," said the pet shop man, "but we do stock a smaller variety. Follow me."

There were quite a lot of baby monsters at the back of the shop. "Some of them grow huge," said the pet shop man.

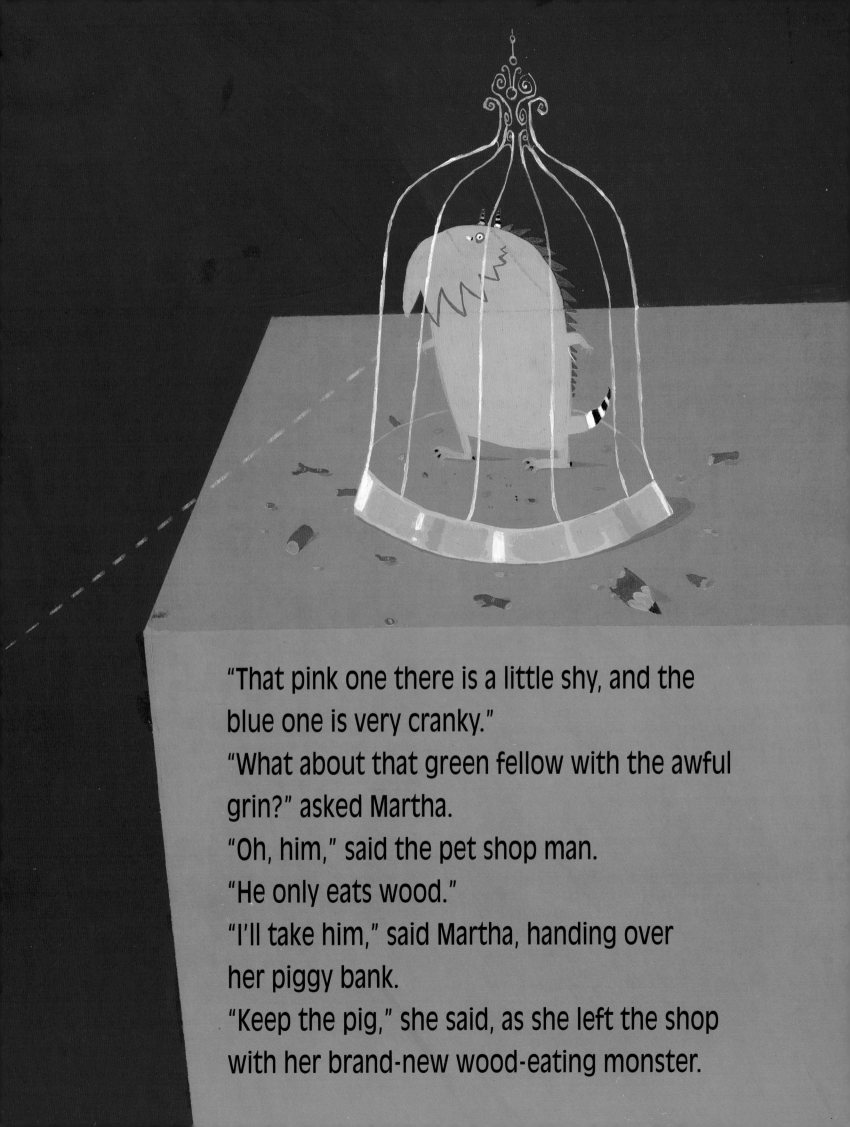

"That pink one there is a little shy, and the blue one is very cranky."

"What about that green fellow with the awful grin?" asked Martha.

"Oh, him," said the pet shop man.

"He only eats wood."

"I'll take him," said Martha, handing over her piggy bank.

"Keep the pig," she said, as she left the shop with her brand-new wood-eating monster.

When she got home, she hid the monster in a shoe box in her bedroom and sneaked out to get his supper—twigs on toast. He devoured them and wanted more.

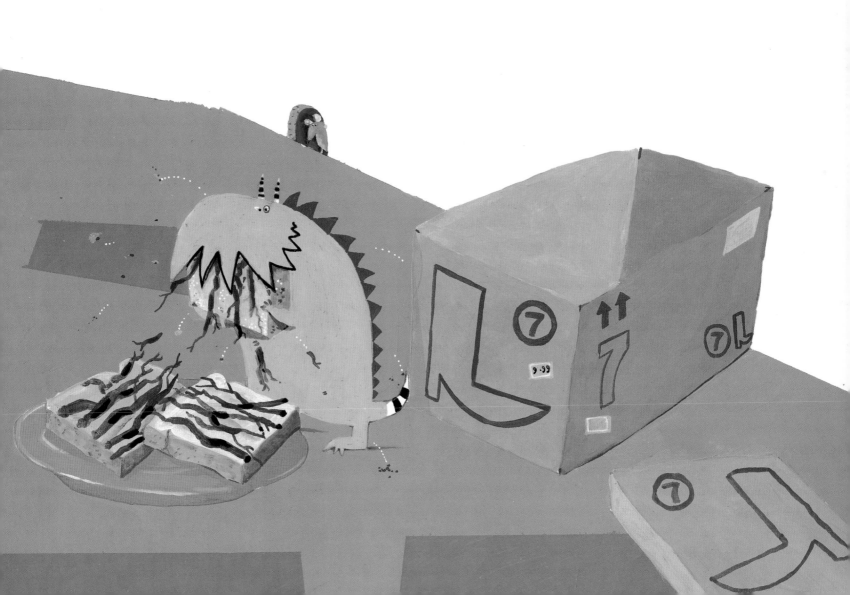

So Martha went back into the yard, sawed some

branches off a tree, and buttered them in the kitchen.

The monster demolished them and demanded more.

This time Martha dismantled the dog's kennel and

spiced the planks with strong pepper.

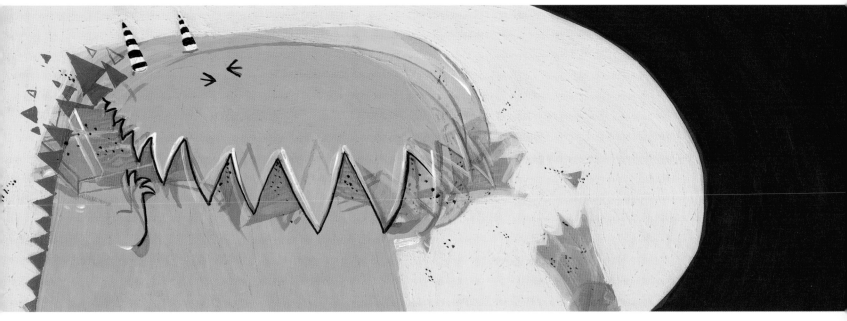

These, too, were guzzled with a grin and a burp.

Things got worse. That night Martha awoke to a terrible crunching, munching sound. She sat up in bed to listen and slid off the edge. The monster had eaten one of the legs! "You greedy thing!" she cried.
"How can I sleep in a three-legged bed?"

He was no longer happy with twigs on toast, buttered branches, or peppered planks. He was too monstrous to fit in a shoe box or a drawer. And there was no "under the bed" left—the monster had eaten the other three legs!

"Tomorrow you go on a diet," said Martha, as she stuffed him into her wardrobe. But it was too late.

Early the next morning, Martha was awakened by a thunderous belch. Her monster was MASSIVE! And her wardrobe was GONE!

"Enough is ENOUGH!"
cried Martha.
She quickly put the monster on a leash and squeezed him
out of the house. They made their way back to the pet shop.

"Excuse me, sir," Martha said to the pet shop man, "but there's a wardrobe in my monster!"

"Oh, dear," he replied, "does he need some coat hangers?"

Martha was furious.
"Don't be funny—and give me a refund!" she yelled.
"Very well," said the pet shop man, "but NO cash."
Martha thought about her sleepy cat, bored goldfish, and dopey dog.

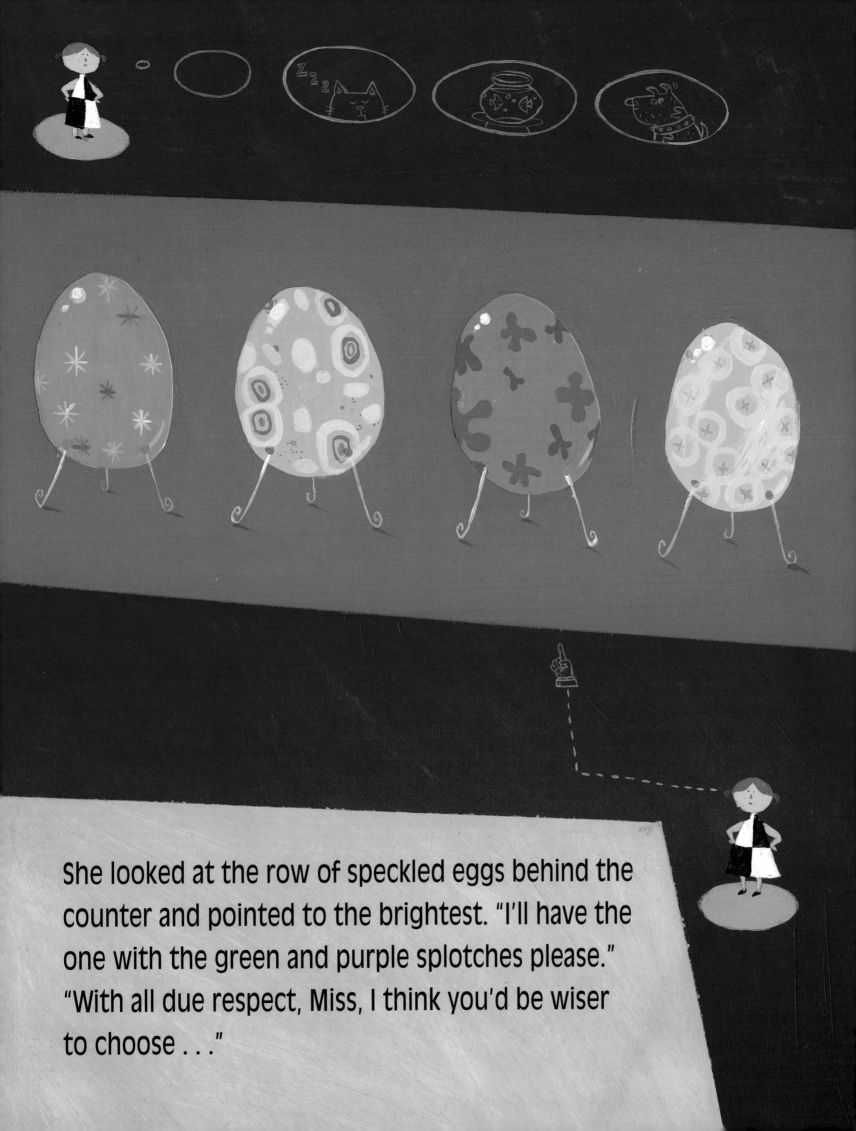

She looked at the row of speckled eggs behind the counter and pointed to the brightest. "I'll have the one with the green and purple splotches please." "With all due respect, Miss, I think you'd be wiser to choose . . ."

Martha thumped her little fist on the counter.
"Now!" she growled.
The man carefully wrapped the egg in tissue paper
and gently placed it in a small cardboard box.
"Thank you," smiled Martha, and off she went.

The pet shop man looked at the monster.
"There's no place for you, Mister Monster, but the backyard,"
he said, and he squeezed the monster out
the back door.

And the monster grinned his most awful grin and had a garden shed for lunch!